AGENTAmelia Hypno Hounds!

AGENT Amelia

Hypno Hounds!

MICHAEL BROAD

Andersen Press
London

First published
in 2008 by
Andersen Press Limited,
20 Vauxhall Bridge Road,
London SW1V 2SA
www.andersenpress.co.uk

Copyright
© Michael Broad, 2008
All rights reserved.

British Library Cataloguing in
Publication Data available.

ISBN 978 184270 816 3

Mixed Sources
Product group from well-managed
forests and other controlled sources
www.fsc.org Cert no. TT-COC-2227
FSC © 1996 Forest Stewardship Council

Printed and bound in Great Britain by
CPI Cox & Wyman, Reading, RG1 8EX

For Lisa

I'M AMELIA KIDD and I'm a secret agent.

Well, I'm not actually a secret agent. I don't work for the government or anything, but I've saved the world loads of times from evil geniuses and criminal masterminds. There are loads of them around if you know what to look for.

I'm really good at disguises. I make my own gadgets (which sometimes work), and I'm used to improvising in sticky situations – which you have to do all the time when you're a secret agent.

These are my Secret Agent Case Files.

The Case of the Hypno Hounds

During the summer, Mum rented a cottage in the countryside for a whole week. I was really looking forward to the calm and quiet, and saw it as a secret agent holiday. A break from saving the world.

Well, that was the plan . . .

As Mum drove along the winding country roads I noticed that we hadn't seen another person for ages,

and as we passed through the village it seemed deserted. I frowned over my sunglasses and decided the countryside was a bit *too* calm and quiet.

In the garden of Shell Cottage I put down my suitcase and looked up at the sign.

'Why is it called *Shell* Cottage?' I wondered aloud.

'Probably because of the seaside,' Mum suggested, and continued up the path.

'Hmmm?' I said, because I'd surveyed the maps in the car and knew the seaside was miles away. You have to do your research when you're a secret agent – even when you're on holiday.

I whipped out my magnifying glass and held it up to the sign to find the 'S' in 'Shell' was newly painted. All the other letters were faded and cracked, which meant the *real* name of the place we were staying was *Hell* Cottage!

When I caught up with Mum she was at the cottage door speaking to a woman who seemed very surprised to see us. She was wearing an apron, which made me think this was probably the housekeeper.

' . . . and you didn't get my letter?' she said. 'The one telling you not to come?'

Mum shook her head and I narrowed my eyes over my sunglasses.

'Then I think you'd better come in,' sighed the woman.

The housekeeper, Mrs Bloom, explained that people were fleeing the village out of sheer terror, and that she'd sent a letter last week urging us not to come for our own safety.

'Why?' Mum and I said together.

'Because the HELL HOUNDS have returned!' she gasped dramatically.

'What's a hell hound?' I asked, as Mum's teacup rattled nervously in her saucer.

'Legend tells of giant beasts who once roamed this countryside,' whispered Mrs Bloom. 'They stood as tall as a man, with massive teeth and big yellow eyes the size of dinner plates!'

Mum's eyes were pretty wide too as she lapped up the story, but I wasn't convinced.

'Have you actually *seen* one of these hell hounds?' I asked casually.

'Well, not exactly,' said Mrs Bloom. 'But I've heard them howling in the night, and found their paw prints in the morning. They were HUGE!'

'Then why do you stay here?' Mum asked, and seemed quite concerned.

'Because I have nowhere else to go,' sighed the woman.

'We'll stay with you,' I said quickly, before Mum had a chance to bundle us back into the car.

Mrs Bloom seemed nice and I wanted to get to the bottom of the hell hounds. 'For the week anyway, eh, Mum?'

'Um, yes, of course!' Mum smiled nervously, reluctant to abandon the poor woman. Mrs Bloom was obviously relieved, and reassured us that it was perfectly safe during the day. She said the hell hounds only come out at midnight, but that the bolts on the doors were very strong.

That night I checked the bolts for myself and then set up a surveillance station at my bedroom window.

 I had binoculars, a flask of orange squash and a packet of biscuits — because night-time surveillance can be hungry work.

As the clock struck midnight, I scanned the surrounding area with my binoculars. The full moon was bright and low and offered some light, but I cursed myself for not pleading harder for night-vision goggles last Christmas.

Then I heard a noise.

'HOOOOOWL!'

The howl seemed quite far off, and was answered by many more.

'HOOOOOWL!' 'HOOOOOWL!'

'HOOOOOWL!'

As each howl grew nearer I suddenly saw a pack of dark shapes charging across the neighbouring field. With the moon behind them it was impossible to see the creatures, but the shadows they cast were long and looked enormous!

When the shadows reached the bushes on the near side of the field there was a frenzied rustling mixed with ferocious growls and snarling. Then the moon disappeared behind the clouds and everything went black.

Uh Oh!

I couldn't see anything through my *non* night-vision binoculars, and I was pretty scared when I heard the creatures prowling in the garden below.

But a secret agent can't let fear get the better of them, so I kept guard over the cottage until the beasts had gone.

In the morning I got up early, crept downstairs and searched the garden for clues. I found lots of trampled flowers and the same huge paw prints the housekeeper had mentioned, but there were no actual leads to go on.

Back indoors, Mrs Bloom was making breakfast, and as Mum was still in bed, I saw this as an opportunity for a bit of informal interrogation.

'Why is this place called Hell Cottage?' I asked casually.

'How did you know that?' gasped the housekeeper.

'Oh, I just notice stuff,' I replied.

'Hell Cottage was the *old* name,' said Mrs Bloom. 'From the days of the legend. But it put people off staying here so I changed it to Shell. Although now the beasts have returned I should probably change it back . . . ' she chuckled nervously, and then burst into tears.

At this point I was certain that Mrs Bloom had nothing to do with the hell hounds. You get a nose for these things when you're a secret agent.

And the distressed housekeeper made me even more determined to solve the midnight mystery.

'Morning!' chirped Mum, skipping cheerily into the kitchen, which meant she'd obviously slept through the howling hell hounds. 'Now, what would you like to do today?'

'I'm afraid most of the local

attractions have closed down,' said Mrs
Bloom, quickly gathering herself. 'But
there is a beautiful nature trail nearby.
Just cut through the field, turn left at
the dogs' home, and then—'

'Dogs' home!' I gasped, realising
this was the lead I was looking for.

'Yes, Polly's Pooches!' said Mrs
Bloom. 'Do you like doggies?'

'Um, yeah!' I said, and turned to
Mum. 'Can we go and see the dogs?'

'Only if you promise not to beg for one like you did last time,' Mum said firmly.

We'd visited a dogs' home last year and I'd pestered Mum to adopt a retired police dog. I thought he'd come in handy as a tracker and sniffer on secret agent missions, but Mum was having none of it.

As we walked across the field I couldn't help wondering why no one else had made the connection between the hell hounds and the dogs' home,

because it seemed pretty obvious to me. This particular mystery was solved the moment we arrived.

Polly's Pooches were all teeny tiny 'handbag' dogs with ribbons in their hair!

Mum didn't have to worry about me begging for a handbag dog. They were all really adorable, but I couldn't keep one in my rucksack because it might chew my gadgets and wee on my disguises.

The dinky dogs were definitely not hell hounds, but there could still be bigger dogs tucked somewhere out of sight. So I gave Mum the slip while she was looking at a rosebush and began snooping around. Eventually, I came upon a large barn that looked like the perfect place to hide a pack of massive dogs!

As I approached, the barn door creaked open and a woman stepped out. This was obviously Polly, of Polly's Pooches, because she had the exact same hairdo as her dogs. I quickly ducked behind the nearest kennel and watched as she bolted the door and fixed it with a padlock. Polly was looking around the whole time to make sure no one was watching, which made her my number one suspect.

When the woman walked away,
I slipped from my hiding place and
approached the barn door. There was
no way I could get inside with the big
padlock in place, but
along the path leading
to the barn I found
loads of paw prints
dried in the mud!

They were the
same huge prints I'd
seen in the cottage
garden!

I followed the tracks with my
magnifying glass and noticed one of
the animals had trailed off towards a
nearby bush, probably to relieve itself.
But when its tracks rejoined the pack
there was a paw print missing, as
though the creature had suddenly lost
a leg!

Animals don't just lose legs willy-nilly, so I pulled out my extendable grabber-hand gadget and began rummaging around in the bush. Then I caught a glimpse of something red and shiny and tugged it from the branches.

It was a Wellington boot!

Hmmm? I thought, and then turned the boot over to find a large paw-shaped mould stuck to the bottom. I pressed the boot into a dried muddy paw print and it was an exact fit.

'YOU THERE!' shrieked a high-pitched voice. 'WHAT ARE YOU DOING?'

I turned to find Polly stomping towards me with a very angry look on her face.

'Hello!' I said cheerily, and quickly booted the boot back into the bush.

'Why are you poking around here?' Polly demanded. 'This area is private property!'

'Er, I got lost,' I sighed, and tried to look like a little girl lost – which is not easy to do in combat trousers. I don't think Polly was convinced, but luckily Mum appeared, providing a handy escape route.

'I've been looking for you everywhere!' she sighed. 'Are you ready to leave?'

'Yes, Mum,' I smiled, skipping past a furious Polly. 'But I'll be back!' I mumbled under my breath.

I didn't pack many disguises for the holiday, so that night I had to borrow Mrs Bloom's cape and crocheted bobble hat. Luckily they were both dark blue and cloaked my almost-midnight dash across the field.

When I reached Polly's barn the door was unbolted, so I poked my head inside and was relieved not to have it bitten off by a pack of massive dogs. The barn was completely empty except for a strange structure at one end, so I slipped inside to take a closer look.

It was a massive cardboard wheel with a whirly pattern painted on the front like a giant lollipop! I stepped up to the structure, turned the wheel a little and then peered around the back.

Behind the wheel there was a table with a map of the whole village with areas coloured in where people had moved out. Most of the map was coloured, in fact Hell Cottage seemed to be the only place left.

Under the map was a blueprint
for a giant dogs' home the exact size
of the village and a diagram for a giant
whirly wheel the size of a football
pitch! None of this made much sense
so I lifted the blueprint to find a
picture of the world cut from an atlas.

It had the words 'I want to take
this over!' scribbled above it.

'Typical!' I thought.

Suddenly I heard someone approaching the barn and quickly crept into the hayloft and hid behind a bale of straw. Moments later Polly barged through the door pushing a wheelbarrow full of Wellington boots, followed by dozens of dinky dogs.

On a whistled command the
animals lined up and waited patiently
as Polly fixed the tall wellies on their
dinky legs, then she stepped away and
spun the giant whirly wheel.

I watched from above as the
cute fluffy pooches stared at the
spinning pattern. They all tilted their
heads as the wheel whizzed round,

then each dog twitched and began
snarling, growling and

HOOOOOWLING!

Polly smiled a wicked smile,
whistled through her fingers and then
flung her arms in the air theatrically.

'Run, my pretties! RUN!' she shrieked, as the mini hell hounds hobbled around and bounded from the barn in their strange red boots, looking scary *and* comical all at the same time.

Evil geniuses and criminal masterminds often like to rant about their plans for world domination. I've heard *loads* of them. And they don't always need an audience, some are quite happy to rant to themselves!

'When my hell hounds have cleared the village,' Polly hissed, pacing up and down like  a lunatic, 'I'll take over the WHOLE WORLD with MILLIONS of hell hounds and a GIANT hypno wheel . . .'

 That explained the village-sized dogs' home. Then I remembered that Hell Cottage was the only place left on the map, which meant the madwoman had probably sent the hounds there. Luckily Polly was too busy ranting to see me climb down from the hayloft and creep away.

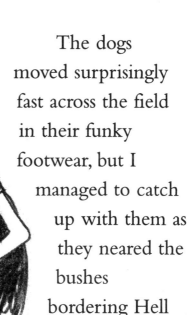

The dogs moved surprisingly fast across the field in their funky footwear, but I managed to catch up with them as they neared the bushes bordering Hell Cottage. The only thing I could think to do was whistle through my fingers like Polly had done, at which point the snarling pooches stopped and hobbled around.

'HOOOOOWL!' 'HOOOOOWL!'

'HOOOOOWL!'

Uh Oh!

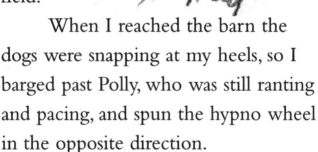

The hell hounds suddenly bounded after me, so I took off back across the field.

When I reached the barn the dogs were snapping at my heels, so I barged past Polly, who was still ranting and pacing, and spun the hypno wheel in the opposite direction.

The dogs hobbled to a halt, tilted their heads, and suddenly turned all cute again.

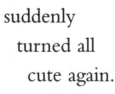

'MY HELL HOUNDS!' yelled
Polly, striding towards me.
'They're not HELL HOUNDS!'
I yelled back. 'They're HANDBAG
HOUNDS!'

'We'll see about that!' she growled, grabbing the other side of the wheel.

Polly tugged the wheel one way while I tugged it back. This tug-of-wheel went on for a quite a long time and as the wheel spun back and forth, the poor dogs sat in the middle of the barn twitching from cute to crazed and crazed to cute.

My arms were getting tired from all the tugging when Polly suddenly let go and leapt around the wheel to grab me, but mid-lunge she happened to glance sideways and froze like a statue. Polly gazed at the hypno wheel, tilted her head and twitched. Then she began snarling, growling and

HOOOOOWLING!

I wasn't sure what to do, so I whistled through my fingers again.

Polly immediately pulled on a pair of wellies, fled the barn and took off across the field like a *human* hell hound. I was about to race after her when I saw the poor pooches peering up at me, and decided to take care of them first.

Luckily the dogs were in cute mode, and to make sure they stayed that way I pulled down the hypno wheel and broke it in half with a well-aimed karate kick. Then I released each of the bewildered beasts from their red Wellington boots.

By the time I reached the cottage I found Mrs Bloom in the garden wielding a broom and shooing Polly out of her flowerbeds. The housekeeper obviously had things under control so I hid behind the hedge until the police arrived to cart Polly away.

She was yelling, 'I'm a HELL HOUND!' and howling at the top of her voice.

You can't take credit for saving the world when you're a secret agent, so when Mrs Bloom went back inside and turned out the lights, I crept through the garden and snuck back into my room.

I tried to look surprised when the housekeeper told us the story the next morning.

'. . . and Polly was sniffing around my rosebushes!' gasped Mrs Bloom. 'So I gave her a good WALLOP with my broom and called the police. And it turned out that *she* was behind the hell hounds! Something to do with welly boot paw prints or something?'

'What a relief!' said Mum.

While I smiled behind my sunglasses.

'Anyway, I've been on the phone all morning and people are already moving back to the village,' added Mrs Bloom, excitedly. 'Oh, and they've asked me to look after the dogs until homes can be found . . .'

'Can I help?' I asked, sitting up eagerly. Because a calm and quiet holiday isn't really for me, I'd rather keep busy. And I'd grown quite fond of those cute little hell hounds. I just had to make sure they stayed away from my rucksack!

The Case of the Sneaky Scientist

I was really looking forward to our first practical science class at school, thinking I'd learn something that could assist my secret agent activities. But the new teacher, Mr Gumble, had other ideas.

'Perfume and stink bombs!' he declared, handing out worksheets to the class.

The girls were given a pink worksheet called *How To Make Perfume*, and the boys were given a blue worksheet called *How to Make a Stink Bomb*. I didn't want to make perfume *or* a stink bomb, so I put my hand up.

'Amelia Kidd?' said Mr Gumble, running his finger down the register.

'Um, is there a worksheet called *How to Make a Smoke Bomb*?' I asked, thinking a smoke bomb might come in handy on secret agent missions, to create a useful diversion or conceal a quick getaway.

The teacher obviously thought I was joking and rolled his eyes disapprovingly.

'A *smoke* bomb!' scoffed Trudy Hart. 'What a typically stupid idea!'

'Oh, mind your own business,' I said.

Trudy is my arch nemesis at school. She's not an evil genius or a criminal mastermind, but she *is* really annoying. Trudy's also very popular and sees herself as a bit of a school celebrity.

'I'm going to create my own perfume called *Love Hart*,' Trudy preened to her surrounding cronies. 'A brand new scent that will smell almost as pretty as me!'

'Then you might want the stink bomb worksheet,' I chuckled.

'Just for that, I'm going to *ban* you from buying it!' snapped Trudy.

'Good!' I said. 'I wouldn't want to smell like *you* anyway—'

'Everyone needs to get into pairs for this project,' interrupted Mr Gumble, glaring at Trudy and me. 'And as you two already have such a dynamic *chemistry*, I think you should make very interesting lab partners.'

'Uh?' I said, as Trudy's jaw dropped.

After the class had shuffled around in a chorus of chair shrieks, each pair were given a measuring beaker and a rack filled with test tubes.

The girls' racks were filled with scented oils and the boys' racks were filled with something murky and unpleasant looking.

Mr Gumble wrote a series of instructions and diagrams on the whiteboard and then explained that one student would do the practical experiment while the other made notes.

'I don't want your fingers contaminating the creation of *Love Hart,* or it might end up smelling of unpopularity,' sniffed Trudy, gathering the apparatus to her side of the desk. 'But I will allow you to make notes while I select the formula.'

'Whatever,' I sighed, thinking science had turned out to be the worst class ever.

'I shall begin with a hint of rose,' said Trudy, lifting a test tube from the rack and waving it under her nose. Then she tipped half of the  oil into the beaker and gazed at it forlornly. 'I think roses will remind everyone of my beautiful rosy cheeks.'

 I was about say something about Trudy's thorny personality, when I noticed Mr Gumble acting very suspiciously at his desk.

He was fiddling inside his very large briefcase and peering over the top to make sure no one was watching.

Uh Oh!

Last week I'd run a background check on Mr Gumble and carried out basic surveillance upon his arrival, as I do with all new teachers. And I'd been particularly vigilant because scientists are really clever and often have thoughts of taking over the world.

At the time, I was convinced the new science teacher was fine and not an evil genius or a criminal mastermind. But judging by his shifty behaviour and the outsized hand luggage, I suspected Mr Gumble had slipped under my radar.

You can't trust scientists!

I was wearing sunglasses under my safety goggles, so Mr Gumble couldn't see me watching as he closed

the case carefully and glanced around the room. He also didn't notice my eyes narrow when he tiptoed through the door clutching his briefcase!

Teachers aren't supposed to leave classrooms unattended unless it's an emergency. Even then, they usually say where they're going and warn the class that the teacher in the next room will be looking in. Mr Gumble just sloped away without a word, which meant he was *definitely* up to something.

'Um, I just need to ask the teacher a question,' I said, slipping out of my seat and rummaging inside my rucksack under the desk. I pulled out the first wig I laid my hands on and tucked it in the back of my combats.

'But who will record my glorious creation?' Trudy demanded.

'Do it yourself, rosy cheeks!' I said, and then legged it after the suspect scientist.

I stepped into the corridor just as Mr Gumble turned the corner, so I sprinted after him and skidded to a halt before the turn. When I peeped around the corner the teacher was hanging up his lab coat and ducking out through the main doors.

Mr Gumble was leaving the school grounds!

I knew I wouldn't get far sneaking out of school looking like a kid, so I grabbed the lab coat and pulled it on. The wig I'd chosen turned out to be frizzy 'disco' hair, but lots of mad scientists have crazy hairdos so I pulled that on too.

Stepping through the school gates I did get a few odd looks from passers-by, but I ignored them and followed Mr Gumble. He was walking very fast, but I'm used to tracking suspects and managed to keep up without being spotted.

The sneaky scientist shot into the local supermarket so I slipped in after him, then we both took trolleys and I made sure to stay low and keep my distance as I followed him through the aisles.

I didn't believe for one minute that the teacher had nipped out of class to do grocery shopping, because he wouldn't need a huge briefcase for that. This made me think that whatever he was up to was probably inside the case!

Mr Gumble stopped in the breakfast cereal aisle, looked around suspiciously and then began loading his trolley with box after box of Sugar Pop Hoops, and he was drawing loads of attention from the other shoppers.

I've been on manoeuvres in a supermarket before, so I know you have to browse and put different stuff in your trolley to pass for a regular shopper.

Watching from behind a box of Oaty Lumps, I realised Mr Gumble was rubbish at deception, but decided I could use this to my advantage and nab the briefcase!

The teacher was becoming more and more flustered as the other shoppers gave him strange looks, so I ran down the aisle with my trolley and positioned myself on the side for a high-speed grab.

Ducking down,
I grabbed for the
briefcase as the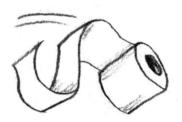
trolley zoomed past, but in
the same moment Mr Gumble
whipped *his* trolley around, causing
me to swerve off course and crash
into the nearest display.

CRASH!

BOING!

BOING!

BOING!

Luckily it was a display of quilted loo rolls that provided a soft, bouncy landing.

Standing up and adjusting my wig I couldn't see Mr Gumble because a crowd had gathered around me making a fuss. I didn't have time for lengthy explanations, so I made use of my disguise.

'Everybody out of the way, I'm
a doctor!' I yelled, and barged through
the crowd.

Running down the aisle, I saw
Mr Gumble leaving the checkout
with four bags of shopping, and when
I say shopping, I mean a dozen boxes
of Sugar Pop Hoops! So I slipped past
the cashier and followed the teacher
back onto the street.

This was turning into a very
complicated mission, but I tried to
stay focused.

If Mr Gumble wasn't planning
anything dodgy *in* the supermarket,
then he was planning something
dodgy with what he'd *bought* from the
supermarket, *and* the contents of his
suspiciously large briefcase . . .
probably.

My suspect was heading back
into school, so I stayed by the gates

and spied through the bars as he
hurried up the path. But instead of
entering the building, he ducked
around the side to where the teachers
park their cars.

I followed using the bushes for
cover and watched as Mr Gumble
opened the boot of his car and began
filling it with Sugar Pop Hoops.

I don't mean he loaded the bags of shopping into the boot – he was actually opening the boxes and *pouring* the cereal, as though the car was a giant breakfast bowl!

CHOMP!

CHOMP!

CHOMP!

From the bushes I could hear chomping sounds coming from the boot, which was bouncing up and down as some mysterious creature fed upon the cereal! I couldn't see what it was, but immediately suspected a diabolical experiment.

Evil scientists can't resist a diabolical experiment.

I had to confront the dodgy Doctor Frankenstein and find out what kind of monster was lurking in his car, but without my trusty rucksack I had no gadgets to defend myself.

When you're a secret agent you have to improvise in sticky situations, so I grabbed the nearest thing that could deliver a good wallop. Unfortunately the nearest thing was a sunflower, but the stem was firm and the head was heavy, and I didn't really have a choice.

I crept along the row of parked vehicles with the uprooted bloom and tiptoed down the side of Mr Gumble's car. With the boot door up the teacher couldn't see me, which was handy, because a girl with a giant flower needs all the cover she can get.

'AHA!' I yelled, leaping into the open and wielding my floral weapon.

'ARGH!' yelled Mr Gumble, hiding behind the Sugar Pop Hoop box.

This wasn't the reaction I was expecting, but I stood my ground.

'I'm not sure *exactly* what you're up to, Gumble,' I said, waving the flower at him. 'But you're not going to get away with it!'

'Amelia Kidd?' frowned the teacher, lowering the cereal box. 'Is that you?'

'Well . . . yes, actually!' I said. My cover was blown, so I pulled the wig off and shoved it in my pocket.

But I wasn't going to let him change the subject that easily. 'As I was saying, I'm here to stop you—'

'And is that my lab coat?' Mr
Gumble asked uncertainly.

'Er, yes,' I said, pulling off the lab
coat and dumping it on the floor.

I couldn't work out what was
going on, because evil geniuses and
criminal masterminds usually turn
pretty nasty when confronted, or they
try to make a quick getaway, or they
start ranting about their fiendish plans.

Mr Gumble just seemed startled and a bit confused.

'Look here!' I yelled, before he could interrupt again. 'I'm here to stop you taking over the world!'

'Taking over the world?' he gasped.

'Yes,' I said, jabbing the sunflower in the direction of the boot. 'You're planning to take over the world using this diabolical monstrosity . . . ' I glanced into the boot for the first time to find a dozen balls of pink fluff peering back at me.

'They're not monsters,' said Mr Gumble, and seemed a bit offended.

'What are they then?' I frowned. 'Man-eating pompoms?'

'I don't know what they are,' Mr Gumble confessed. 'They grew by accident in my lab. But they don't eat people,' he added quickly, waving the cereal box. 'They eat Sugar Pop Hoops.'

I propped my sunflower against
the car, reached cautiously into the
boot and picked up one of the small
fluffy creatures. It was warm in my
hand and giggled when I tickled its
fur.

'My wife usually looks after them, but she's visiting her mother,' explained Mr Gumble. 'So I had to bring them to school for their morning feed. You see we have no children of our own and have grown awfully fond of them . . . '

'Can I feed them?' I asked. Mr Gumble shrugged and handed me the last box of Sugar Pop Hoops. 'When the scientific world discovers that I've accidentally created a new species, they'll want to take them away,' he said sadly. 'They'll put them in a cage and poke and prod them . . . '

'You can't trust scientists,' I said, shaking the cereal into the boot. The pink fluffy creatures jumped up and down excitedly as they chomped on their food. 'But how will they find out you have them?'

'When you tell people, of course,' said Mr Gumble. 'Word will spread very quickly.'

'Oh, I won't tell anyone,' I said casually.

'You won't?' gasped the teacher.

'No,' I said, realising that my initial assessment of Mr Gumble had been correct and that he wasn't an evil genius or a criminal mastermind. 'As long as you promise not to take over the world with them.'

'Why would I want to take over the world?' he frowned.

'I don't know,' I said. 'But I've met a *lot* of people who do . . . '

I suddenly realised I'd said too much, and for a moment it looked as though Mr Gumble was about to quiz me about *my* part in all this. But then he nodded and smiled kindly.

'I promise not to take over the world,' he said, holding out his hand.

As we shook hands to seal the deal I could tell the teacher and I had an understanding.

I wouldn't mention his adopted pompoms and he wouldn't mention my secret agent activities.

With the fluffy creatures fed, Mr Gumble opened his large briefcase and they jumped in one by one, while I gathered the empty cereal boxes and stuffed them in the shopping bags for recycling.

Then the teacher pulled on his lab coat and led me back to class.

The science room was very different from the one we'd left behind!

Standing in the doorway, the
first difference I noticed was the noise,
because all of my classmates were
yelling and screaming. The second
difference was the smell, which was
REALLY bad. It reminded me of
rotten eggs and mouldy cabbage, mixed
with the occasional whiff of perfume.

'SILENCE!' roared an angry
voice behind us.

Mr Gumble and I jumped as the
head teacher, Mrs Marshall, barged
past and stormed into the classroom.
Then everything immediately went
quiet – but still smelled like a cesspit.

'What on earth is going on in
here?' Mrs Marshall demanded,

scanning the room and then turning
to Mr Gumble for the answer. 'I saw
you strolling down the corridor and
can only assume you have an excellent
excuse for leaving the classroom
unattended?'

I looked up at Mr Gumble, who had a familiar startled expression on his face. It was the same expression he wore when I confronted him with the sunflower, and I could tell he was about to confess again!

I didn't want the pompoms to get poked and prodded so I quickly spoke up.

'It was an *emergency*, Mrs Marshall!' I gasped, remembering the rule about unattended classrooms.

Then I remembered I was still holding the carrier bag filled with empty cereal boxes. 'I ate too many Sugar Pop Hoops and was sick!'

'Oh,' said the head teacher, taking the bag and peering inside.

'Oh, dear!'

Mrs Marshall bought the story and left Mr Gumble in charge. The teacher gave me a grateful nod as he placed the briefcase carefully on his desk, and then took control of the classroom.

I went back to my seat next to Trudy and lifted the beaker of *Love Hart* to my nose.

'URGH!' I shuddered. 'Is *this* what you smell like?'

'Of course not, you unpopular fool!' growled Trudy, glaring at me as though everything was my fault. 'The boys poured something *else* into the beaker, something that smelled like manure!'

'Well, manure *is* very good for roses,' I smiled, looking at Trudy's furious face, which was now scarlet with rage. 'Perhaps that explains why your rosy cheeks are positively blooming!'

The Case of the Terrible Teddies

'I just can't understand why you're still sulking about it!' said Mum, as we entered the local department store.

'We're here now, and it's not as though you're likely to *need* anything.'

'Hmph!' I said, folding my arms defiantly.

We'd spent the whole car journey arguing about my rucksack. Mum insisted that it was too big and heavy for a shopping trip, and I'd failed to offer a good enough reason why I needed it.

I couldn't tell Mum the bag was full of secret agent stuff or that you never know when an evil genius or criminal mastermind might try to take over the world. So my faithful rucksack got left behind.

'Now, what is it we're looking for again?' Mum asked cheerily, keen to change the subject. 'A teddy bear and a pair of roller skates?'

'Turbo Ted,' I sighed. 'A remote-control teddy bear *on* roller skates.'

'Oh, yes,' Mum smirked, 'I remember now . . .'

Mum hadn't *really* forgotten – she was just trying to get me talking.

My cousin had been going on and on all week about getting Turbo Ted for his birthday. It was the latest toy craze for younger kids.

Unfortunately, when we found the Turbo Ted display it was empty. There was not a single bear for sale and loads of disappointed kids gathered around. One of the disappointed kids was much bigger than the rest, and was making a much bigger fuss!

'THIS IS UNACCEPTABLE!'
she squealed.

Trudy Hart was standing next to
the display with her weary looking
dad, and she was causing a bit of a
scene. The store manager was trying to
calm her down but without much
success.

'I'm terribly sorry, miss,' he said. 'But we do have many other nice things for a sophisticated young lady. I'm sure you're too grown up to play with teddy bears anyway ...'

Trudy's dad gasped and took a step back.

'I don't *play* with them, you silly little man,' growled Trudy. 'I collect them!'

'Oh,' gulped the manager. 'I'm sure I didn't mean ...'

'It's a very *grown-up* and intellectual hobby,' interrupted Trudy. 'My teddy bear collection is one of the finest in the world, and you've just ruined my reputation with your incompetcnce!'

With this Trudy stormed away, leaving the manager with his mouth hanging open.

'Those roller-skating teddies must be awfully popular to sell out so quickly,' said Mum, stepping up to the manager. 'Do you have any idea when they'll be back in stock?'

'That's the problem, madam,' he said, scratching his head. 'Fifty new Turbo Teds arrived this morning and we haven't sold a single one! The entire stock just vanished!'

I dipped my sunglasses when I heard the word 'vanished', because in my experience things never just vanish. There's always *someone* behind the vanishing.

'You mean they were stolen?' I asked casually.

'No,' said the manager. 'The head of security has been through all the CCTV tapes and said the bears were there one minute and gone the next. It's a complete mystery!'

Hmmm? I thought.

I was just wondering whether the missing teddies warranted an investigation when I saw something whiz by out of the corner of my eye.

I only caught a brief glimpse, but it looked suspiciously like a small bear on roller skates!

'I suppose we'll have to find something else for your cousin,' Mum sighed, as the store manager wandered off. 'I know he'll be disappointed, but I'm sure if we put our heads together we can think of something nice.'

I frowned at the 'we' part, because I couldn't carry out an investigation with Mum tagging along. And I knew she'd come and find me if I gave her the slip, so I needed a really good excuse to go off on my own.

'Can I go and have a look in the Girly Girl clothing section?' I asked, knowing Mum would definitely encourage my showing an interest in pretty dresses instead of the usual combat gear.

'Yes, of course!' Mum gasped, flapping her hands eagerly. 'Off you go, darling!'

I immediately took off down the aisle towards the girls' section. Without my rucksack I was planning to dress up in a pink frilly dress and bonnet disguise. It would be uncomfortable, but Mum wouldn't recognise me and no one would suspect a girly girl of being a secret agent.

Unfortunately I had to abandon
that plan the moment I arrived at
Girly Girl.

'Well, I think they're all UGLY!'
yelled a familiar voice amid a sea of
frills and bows. 'I wouldn't be seen
dead in any of them, and I think
you'll find the customer is *always*
right!'

I'd managed to avoid a confrontation with Trudy Hart back at the bear display, and I definitely didn't have time for one now. So I ducked into the nearest aisle and found myself in the *men's* clothing section!

A secret agent can't afford to be choosy when they need a quick disguise, so I rummaged through the racks for something I could work with. Eventually I pulled on a brown macintosh, popped a bowler hat on my head and grabbed an umbrella.

A quick glance in the mirror revealed a rather convincing 'city gent'.

I was adjusting my bowler, which was a bit too big, when I heard a commotion at the check out. The queuing customers were searching their pockets and handbags while the store staff looked bewildered.

'My wallet!' said one man.

'My purse!' said a woman.

It looked as though most of the customers in the queue had lost their money, which was a lot of picked pockets for one department store. This meant there would have to be a whole gang of pickpockets working the place, which was a bit of a coincidence considering the missing Turbo Teds.

Unless . . .

I scanned the store and saw a small furry paw reach into a lady's handbag and pull out her purse! Nearby another paw appeared from a clothes rack and reached into a man's coat. In fact everywhere I looked I saw little furry arms in pockets and handbags, and brown blurs whizzing all over the place.

The Turbo
Teds were robbing
the place!

One of the bears whizzed
past my legs with a pink purse in its
paws, so I took off after it, chasing it
through the aisles as
its fuzzy brown
legs skated like
mad. As the toy
weaved in and out of
clothes racks it was getting away, so I
leapt forward, swung my brolly and
hooked the cuddly
crook around
the waist.

'Gotcha!' I said, and immediately flicked the switch on its back to 'OFF'.

Then I plucked the purse from its paws and inspected the fuzzy bandit. I suspected someone had programmed the toys and sent them on a stealing spree, but there were no marks or obvious modifications – it looked like a regular Turbo Ted.

A regular *remote-controlled* Turbo Ted!

Which meant someone was *controlling* the burglar bears from a distance.

The department store was massive and full of people moving around, so trying to spot a dodgy character among the masses was like finding a needle in a haystack. Then I looked up and saw a security camera buzzing over my head.

'Aha!' I said, shoving the bear headfirst into the clothes rack.

The manager said the security guard hadn't seen the stock disappear, but then he wasn't a secret agent with an eye for evil geniuses and criminal masterminds. If I could just find a way to view those CCTV tapes . . .

'THIEF!' shrieked a familiar voice. 'That short man has my pretty pink purse!'

Uh Oh!

I quickly whipped the brolly handle under my nose to conceal my face from Trudy, but before I could scarper, the store manager appeared from behind and grabbed my arm firmly.

'Gotcha!' he said, taking the purse and handing it to my fuming foe.

Trudy snatched the purse and looked as though she was about to give the manager another telling-off, when I suddenly worked out how I could get in to see the security tapes. I quickly fished around in my pocket and pulled out my library card.

'Excellent work!' I said, in my deepest, most official voice. 'Very well done!'

'Excuse me?' said the manager.

'I'm the Regional, er, Security Supervisory, er, Manager!' I said waving my library card in his face. 'I got a call from headquarters saying you have a security problem in your store?'

'Well, yes,' frowned the manager. 'But—'

'No time to explain,' I said, pocketing the card and tugging my arm free. 'You must take me to your head of security immediately!'

'But what about me?' Trudy demanded. 'I'm a victim of crime!'

'Pardon me, miss,' I said. 'You dropped your purse over by the frilly knickers and I was simply attempting to return it. Perhaps you should spend more time guarding your possessions and less time yelling at people!'

The store manager stifled a smirk as he led me to the security guard's office, where he introduced me as the Regional Security Supervisory Manager, which was handy because I'd forgotten the made-up title I'd given him.

'So you need to view the tapes?' said the head of security after the manager left.

'Yes,' I said, officiously. 'Start with the Turbo Ted display from earlier today.'

The man fiddled with a couple of buttons on the consul and then pointed to one of the monitors. But instead of the teddy display, the screen showed a close up of the men's

clothing section, with me assembling my city gent disguise!

Uh Oh!

It was then that I took a closer look at the joysticks lined up along his desk. At first I'd assumed they were there to operate the CCTV cameras, but on closer inspection I realised they were not actually connected to anything. They were *remote control* joysticks!

'You're working the cuddly crooks!' I said, annoyed that I hadn't worked it out earlier. 'And you're using the security cameras in the store to direct them from a distance!'

'Yes,' said the security guard, proudly. 'And this is only the beginning!'

'Whatever do you mean?' I gasped, knowing exactly what he meant. I can usually tell when a 'taking over the world' rant is coming and I had to stall for time while I worked out a plan.

'Once my bears have stolen enough purses and wallets, I'll buy an army of Turbo Teds,' he said, pointing to the paused pickpockets on the monitors. 'And soon I'll have enough to rob the whole world!'

'You won't get away with it!' I said.

'Oh, yes, I will!' he laughed, and then began tugging and jerking the joysticks.

At first I thought he was ignoring me and carrying on with the pick-pocketing, which would have been a bit rude. Then I heard a strange noise thundering down the corridor and realised he'd recalled the bears to the office!

The rumbling reached the room with a screech of wheels and the door burst open. Then fifty fluffy bears zoomed inside with wallets and purses and began circling my legs like I was a human roundabout.

ZOOM!

ZOOM!

ZOOM!

The security guard leapt up, snatched the loot from each of the bears and stuffed it in a sack. Then he threw the sack over his shoulder, laughed like a maniac and bolted from the office.

The Turbo Teds had picked up quite a speed which meant I couldn't step through them, so I pulled off my macintosh and threw it over the toy tornado. Most of the bears became tangled in the coat, careered across the room and landed in a heap against the wall.

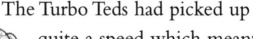

The rest I could hook
away using my brolly
like a hockey stick. WHACK!

WHACK!

WHACK!

I ran to the camera consul and
saw the security guard walking very
quickly through the store, but not so
quickly as to draw attention to himself.
Then I noticed there were still a few
bears in the store so I began wiggling
the joysticks to get them to move.

Once I'd worked out the correct
joysticks I sent the skaters after the
guard, weaving them in and out of his
legs. The bears slowed him down but
he was still getting away, so I took off
after him.

Back in the store I realised I was no longer in disguise, the coat and brolly were in the office and all I had left was the bowler hat – which must have looked pretty odd on its own, so I slipped it off.

I ducked down as I ran through the aisles, because I couldn't risk drawing attention to myself dressed as me, but the guard was nearing the exit doors and if I didn't act fast he would escape with the loot.

I couldn't shout out because no one would suspect a security guard of picking pockets, and I had no rucksack – which meant no gadgets to assist me.

All I had was a silly bowler hat that wasn't even mine . . .

Hmmm? I thought, and paused to turn the bowler hat over in my hands.

As I suspected there was an electronic security tag on the inside rim, which meant no one could take it from the store because alarms would go off if it passed through the sensors!

With the guard approaching the exit doors I knew I only had one shot, so I weighed the bowler in my hand, made a few practice flicks with my wrist and then threw the hat like a Frisbee.

The bowler flew through the air like a black flying saucer, soaring over the heads of the shoppers and gliding through the sensors as the guard approached. It was a better shot than I'd hoped for because it clipped his head and knocked the peak cap over his eyes.

WA! WA! WA!

The store alarms screamed and all the shoppers turned to see the guard bump blindly into the doors before staggering back into the store. Just then a stray bear rolled under his legs and sent the crook off balance until he landed on his bottom.

'My wallet!' yelled one man.

'My purse!' shrieked a woman.

The loot sack had fallen open, spilling its contents over the floor. A crowd of angry shoppers quickly gathered around the crook and moments later the store manager appeared and pulled the guard to his feet.

'Has anyone seen the Regional Security Supervisory Manager?' he asked. 'Short chap, with a brolly and a bowler?'

Needless to say no one had seen him, so the store manager called the police and the dazed guard was taken away. He was mumbling about little girls and bears, which didn't make any sense to anyone.

As the crowd dispersed with their purses and wallets, Trudy stormed towards the manager with her dad in tow. She picked up the stray Turbo Ted that had tripped the crook and waved it at him angrily.

'So you had them in stock the whole time!' she growled.

'Er, I'm not sure where this one came from,' said the manager, frowning at the bear.

'But I'd be happy to let you have it, to apologise for any inconvenience. I'm sure we can find the joystick . . . '

'Are you completely MAD?' Trudy squealed. 'It's worth NOTHING if it's not still in the box!'

Trudy Hart stomped out of the department store, and she left without ever knowing I was there, because this time I was hiding behind a rack of puffy meringue dresses with matching frilly bloomers.

'There you are!' said Mum, stepping through the aisle. 'Did you find anything you like?'

'No!' I gasped, backing away from the dresses before she insisted on buying one.

'Me neither,' Mum sighed. 'It's such a shame about those roller skating bears . . . '

'THE TURBO TEDS?' I yelled, loud enough for the manager to hear.

'IF ONLY THEY HAD *ONE* IN STOCK! I'M SURE WE DON'T CARE IF IT'S IN A BOX OR NOT ...'

Mum had obviously missed all the drama and didn't understand why I was speaking so loud. So I just raised an eyebrow and tried to look surprised when the manager made his way towards us.

He was smiling and holding up my cousin's birthday present.

Watch out for my other books

AGENT Amelia

Three more fabulously funny
stories in each

AGENT AMELIA: Ghost Diamond!
ISBN 9781842706626 £4.99

AGENT AMELIA: Zombie Cows!
ISBN 9781842706633 £4.99